This Little Tiger book belongs to:

_____

_____

_____

_____

For Daniel
~*J.S.*

For Chris and Sal's new baby
~*J.C.*

LITTLE TIGER PRESS
An imprint of Magi Publications
1 The Coda Centre, 189 Munster Road
London SW6 6AW
www.littletigerpress.com
This paperback edition published in 2002
First published in Great Britain 2002
Text © 2002 Julie Sykes • Illustrations © 2002 Jane Chapman
Julie Sykes and Jane Chapman have asserted their rights to
be identified as the author and illustrator of this work under
the Copyright, Designs and Patents Act, 1988.
Printed in Belgium
LTP/1300/0063/0110
All rights reserved • ISBN 978-1-85430-772-9
3 5 7 9 10 8 6 4

DORA'S CHICKS

by Julie Sykes   *illustrated by* Jane Chapman

LITTLE TIGER PRESS
London

One morning, Dora opened her eyes.

Her six fluffy chicks were beginning to stir.

"My chicks will be hungry," clucked Dora.

"I'd better go and look for their breakfast."

Dora hopped out of the hen house
and into the yard. She was only gone
for a minute, but when she came back,
the hen house was empty!
"Where are my six chicks?" cried Dora.

Quickly, Dora ran back into the farmyard
and over to the pigsty.
"Hello, Penny," she called. "I've lost my
chicks. Have you seen them?"
"Sorry, Dora, I'm feeding my piglets.
I haven't had time to notice
where your chicks have gone,"
oinked Penny.

Dora watched the piglets
rushing towards their mother.
But who was that following
them?

It was one of her chicks!
"Stop!" she clucked. "Chicks
don't suckle for their food."

Dora hopped after her chick and rescued it before it got trampled. "One chick safe," said Dora, feeling a little happier. "But that leaves five to find."

Dora and her one chick went down to the pond.
Doffy Duck was there, getting her ducklings into line.
"Hello, Doffy," called Dora. "I've lost some chicks.
Have you seen them?"
"I'm teaching my ducklings to fish for their food,"
quacked Doffy. "I haven't had time to see where your
chicks have gone."

Dora watched the ducklings splash into
the water. The last one couldn't keep up.
Suddenly, Dora realised it wasn't a
duckling at all . . .

It was another of her chicks!
"Wait!" cried Dora. "Chicks don't
fish for food. They can't swim!"

Dora chased after her chick, and only just
stopped it from jumping into the water.
"Two chicks safe," said Dora, feeling quite
pleased. "But that leaves four to find."

Dora continued on her search. On the way past the big barn she stopped to look inside. Honey Horse was showing her foal how to eat hay. "Hello, Honey," called Dora. "I've lost some chicks. Have you seen them?" "Sorry, Dora, but I'm far too busy with my foal to notice chicks," neighed Honey.

Sadly, Dora hopped back
towards the door.
But who was that, climbing
the haystack?

"*Two* of my chicks," cried Dora with relief. Quickly, she rescued them before they slipped and fell. "Chicks don't eat hay," said Dora, as she chivvied her brood over to the door.

Back in the sunlight, Dora counted
her chicks.
"One, two, three, four. But I have six
chicks, so there are still two missing."

Dora searched everywhere for her last two chicks.
She searched in the yard, and she searched in the
orchard. She squeezed under the gate . . .

and saw Ringo Robin on the other side of
the lane, pulling up worms to eat.
"Cheep, cheep, cheep," cried Dora's chicks,
feeling hungry. "We want breakfast!"

Dora was just about to turn back,
when she saw . . .

her fifth chick crossing the lane
to reach Ringo and his worms.
"Don't move!" ordered Dora.
"You must *never* cross a road
without looking both ways
first. You might get hurt."

Ringo flew over to see
what all the fuss was about.
"Goodness, what a lot
of chicks," he exclaimed.
"Yes," said Dora. "But I
have *six* chicks, so one is
still missing."

Dora and her chicks hopped through
the top field.
They flapped across the bottom field.

They passed the cowshed and the dog kennel. And all the time, Dora kept looking for her sixth chick.

The other five chicks were tired. "We're hungry," they complained. At last Dora knew she must take the chicks home and feed them.

Sadly, she headed back to the hen house.
The little chicks hurried after her.
"Cheep, cheep, cheep," they cried.
"Breakfast!"
Dora saw the grain scattered in the yard,
but she didn't feel hungry.
"Where is my sixth chick?" she clucked.

"Here I am!" cheeped a tiny voice.
Dora's sixth chick was already back
in the yard, tucking into breakfast!
Happy tears splashed from Dora's eyes.
At last all her chicks were home again.

"Excuse me, Dora, can you help me?
I need to find some moss for my nest."
It was Ringo Robin.
"I'm sorry, Ringo," said Dora. "But I'm
far too busy looking after my six chicks."